My First Nursery Book

Drawings by
Franciszka Themerson

Published in association with Tate Publishing
Abrams Books for Young Readers, New York

Who killed Cock Robin?
   "I," said the Sparrow,
   "With my bow and arrow;
I killed Cock Robin."

Who saw him die?
"I," said the Fly,
"With my little eye;
I saw him die."

W

ho caught his blood?
  "I," said the Fish,
  "With my little dish;
I caught his blood."

Who'll make his shroud?
"I," said the Beetle,
"With my little needle;
I'll make his shroud."

Who'll be the parson?
   "I," said the Rook,
   "With my little book;
   I'll be the parson."

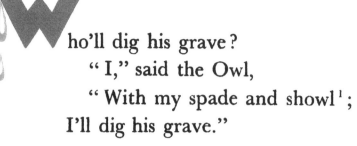Who'll dig his grave?
   "I," said the Owl,
   "With my spade and showl[1];
I'll dig his grave."

[1] 'Showl' is an old word for shovel.

Who'll be the clerk?
"I," said the Lark,
"If it's not in the dark;
I'll be the clerk."

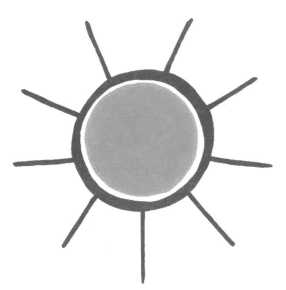

Who'll carry him to the grave?
　"I," said the kite,
　　"If it's not in the night;
I'll carry him to the grave."

Who'll carry the link[1]?
  " I," said the Linnet,
  " I'll fetch it in a minute ;
I'll carry the link."

[1] Torch.

Who'll be chief mourner?
  " I," said the Dove,
  " I mourn for my love ;
I'll be chief mourner."

Who'll bear the pall?
"We," said the Wren,
Both the cock and the hen;
"We'll bear the pall."

Who'll sing a psalm?
"I," said the Thrush,
As she sat in a bush;
"I'll sing a psalm."

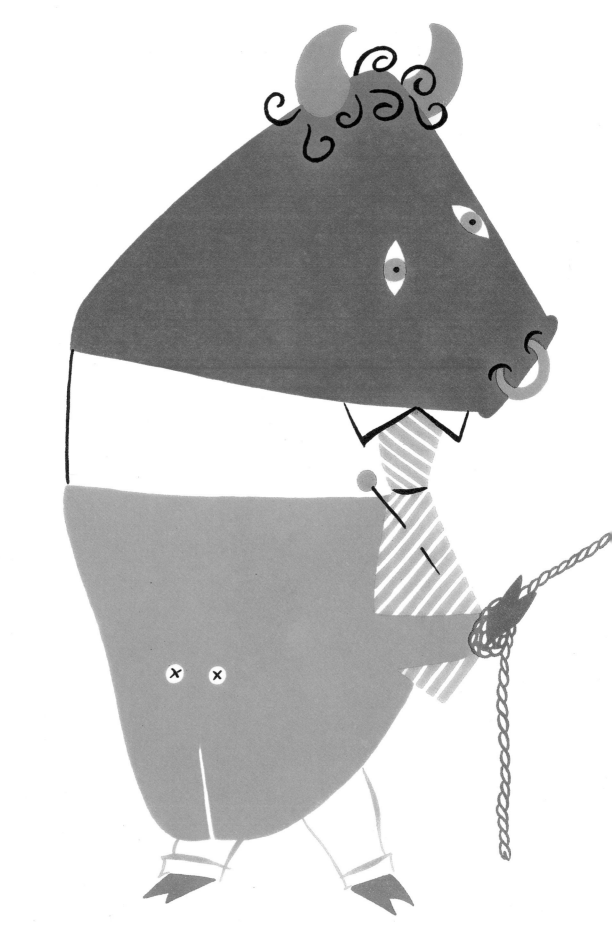

Who'll toll the bell?
   "I," said the Bull,
   "Because I can pull;
I'll toll the bell."

All the birds of the air
   Fell a-sighing and a-sobbing,
When they heard the bell toll
   For poor Cock Robin.

THE GINGERBREAD MAN

A Little Old Lady

Once took a flat pan
And made for her husband
A Gingerbread Man.

The strange little man was made in this wise,
He had almonds for fingers, and currants for eyes ;
He was dressed in the brownest of brown little suits,
With little brown trousers and tiny brown boots.

As the man to her husband the old lady bore,
He suddenly jumped from the pan to the floor,
And scampered as fast as his little brown feet
Would carry him into the quaint little street.

The old lady's husband,
Who wanted a bite,
Ran out to prevent
Mr Gingerbread's flight.

The good wife came after,
But quicker than she
Was a brisk little dog
Who was out for a spree.

The little brown man cared never a pin;
He ran past the dog, crying out with a grin
(While doggie barked loudly and on they all ran):
" You cannot catch me, I'm the Gingerbread Man!"

The little old lady ran well in the hunt;
And so did her husband, with doggie in front;
But the Gingerbread Man laughed aloud in his glee:
" Though you all may be clever, you cannot catch me!"

A big tabby cat
With a very fierce face
Saw Gingerbread coming
And took up the chase.

A sturdy policeman,
Slow pacing his beat,
Fell in with the others
And raced down the street.

The little brown man ran quicker and quicker;
The crowd at his heels grew thicker and thicker;
All shouted as loud as they could while they ran:
" Stop thief!   He's a runaway Gingerbread Man!"

They chased him for many and many a mile,
But Gingerbread Man ran in wonderful style.
Sighed the p'liceman, " I wonder if ever we can
Catch up with this fleet-footed Gingerbread man."

A dapper young soldier
Next took up the chase,
Though nothing he knew
Of the facts of the case.

Then a horse, with a neigh,
Bounded into the throng,
And with clattering hoofs
Galloped madly along.

Uphill and downhill the race did not pause,
For all were determined to stick to the cause ;
With ease did the Gingerbread Man keep ahead,
But many behind him were very near dead.

They dashed into valleys ; they raced over hills ;
They splashed into cool little silvery rills ;
They climbed over gates, and they leapt over stiles ;
They ran and they shouted for hundreds of miles.

A gentle old cow,
By the noise frantic sent,
Rushed into the crowd,
Raising dust as she went.

And a cunning old crow
Left his favourite tree,
To follow the chase
With the greatest of glee.

On through the country, and on through the towns;
On through the forests, and over the downs;
And when he looked back at the hurrying crowd
The little brown man felt exceedingly proud!

The dog and the cat, the horse and the cow,
The crow and the soldier, were all panting now;
The little old lady was weary indeed,
Although she kept on at a marvellous speed.

A sleepy-eyed owl
Woke and stared at the sight,
Then spreading his wings
Joined Jim Crow in the flight.

Some threshers at work
In a barnyard with flails
Took quick to their heels
And leapt over the rails.

But though the crowd grew, and increased as time went,
The little brown man seemed extremely content,
And laughed as he saw how they all ran and ran
And yet couldn't catch him—the Gingerbread Man.

He capered in frolic, he shouted with glee :
" For all you're so many, you cannot catch me !
Although you are running as fast as you can,
I'm faster, for I am the Gingerbread Man ! "

Some mowers were mowing
A meadow hard by,
But couldn't resist
The hue and the cry.

What shrieking and shouting arose as they sped
In chase of the man made of sweet gingerbread !
Some fell on their faces, hard pushed from behind,
But picked themselves up, and not one seemed to mind.

The threshers, the mowers, the horse, and the crow
Were all out of breath, but continued to go,
But the dog and the cat, although hot, did the best,
And ran, with their tongues out, in front of the rest.

In fact with such zeal and such vigour they ran
They might have caught up with the Gingerbread Man;
When, all of a sudden, he turned to the right,
Scrambled over a wall, and was lost to their sight.

But there was a river
With rushes and rocks,
And high on the bank sat
A cunning old fox.

" Oh, where are you going, my Gingerbread Man ? "
Asked the fox.   " I will help you along if I can.
Although I'm a fox I can swim like a fish,
And will take you across on my back if you wish."

The little brown man thanked the fox with a bow,
And said, " If you're ready I'll go with you now."
He jumped on his muzzle in less than a trice . . .
But foxes are cunning and ginger is nice.

    And Gingerbread vanished
    In less than a twink.
    Now where did he go to ? . . .
    I leave you to think !

THREE little pigs

 nce upon a time there was an old sow with three little pigs, and as she had not enough to keep them she sent them out to seek their fortune.

he first that went off met a man with a bundle of straw, and said to him: "Please, man, give me that straw to build me a house!" Which the man did, and the little pig built a house with it.

Presently along came a wolf, knocked at the door, and said:

"Little pig, little pig, let me come in."

To which the pig answered:

"No, no, by the hair of my chinny chin chin."

The wolf then answered to that:

"Then I'll huff and I'll puff, and I'll blow your house in."

So he huffed and he puffed, and he blew his house in, and ate up the little pig.

The second little pig met a man with a bundle of furze, and said:

"Please, man, give me that furze to build a house."

Which the man did, and the pig built his house.

hen along came the wolf and said :

"Little pig, little pig, let me come in."

"No, no, by the hair of my chinny chin chin."

"Then I'll puff and I'll huff, and I'll blow your house in."

So he huffed, and he puffed, and he puffed, and he huffed, and at last he blew the house down, and he ate up the second pig.

he third little pig met a man with a load of bricks, and said:

"Please, man, give me those bricks to build a house with."

So the man gave him the bricks, and he built his house with them. So the wolf came, as he did to the other little pigs, and said:

"Little pig, little pig, let me come in."

"No, no, by the hair of my chinny chin chin."

"Then I'll huff, and I'll puff, and I'll blow your house in."

Well, he huffed and he puffed, and he huffed and he puffed, and he puffed, and he huffed; but he could *not* get the house down.

When he found that he could not, with all his huffing and puffing, blow the house down, he said:

"Little pig, I know where there is a nice field of turnips."

"Where?" said the little pig.

"Oh, in Mr Smith's home field, and if you will be ready to-morrow morning I will call for you, and we will go together and get some for dinner."

"Very well," said the little pig, "I will be ready. What time do you mean to go?"

"Oh, at six o'clock."

Well, the little pig got up at five and got the turnips before the wolf came (which he did about six).

When the wolf did come, at six, he said :

" Little pig, are you ready ? "

The little pig said :

" Ready ! I have been and come back again, and got a nice potful for dinner."

The wolf felt very angry at this, but thought that he would get even with the little pig somehow or other, so he said :

" Little pig, I know where there is a nice apple-tree."

" Where ? " said the pig.

" Down at Merry Garden," replied the wolf, " and if you will not deceive me I will come for you at five o'clock to-morrow and we will go together and get some apples."

Well, the little pig bustled up next morning at four o'clock, and went off for the apples; hoping to get back before the wolf came; but he had further to go, and had to climb the tree, so that just as he was coming down from it, he saw the wolf coming, which as you may suppose, frightened him very much.

When the wolf came up he said :

"Little pig, what!—are you here before me? Are they nice apples?"

"Yes, very," said the little pig, "I will throw you down one."

And he threw it so far that, while the wolf was gone to pick it up, the little pig jumped down, and ran home.

The next day the wolf came again and said to the little pig:

"Little pig, there is a fair at Shanklin this afternoon. Will you go?"

"Oh, yes," said the pig, "I will go. What time shall you be ready?"

"At three," said the wolf.

So the little pig went off before the time as usual, and got to the fair and bought a butter churn, which he was going home with, when he saw the wolf coming. Then he could not tell what to do. So he got into the churn to hide, and by so doing turned it round, and it rolled down the hill with the pig in it, which frightened the wolf so much that he ran home without going to the fair.

He went to the little pig's house and told him how frightened he had been by a great round thing which came down the hill past him. Then the little pig said:

"Ha! I frightened you, then. I had been to the fair and bought a butter churn, and when I saw you I got into it and rolled down the hill."

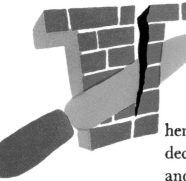

hen the wolf was very angry indeed, and declared he *would* eat up the little pig, and that he would get down the chimney after him. When the little pig saw what he was about, he hung on the pot, full of water, and made up a blazing fire, and, just as the wolf was coming down, took off the cover, and in fell the wolf; so the little pig put on the cover again in an instant, boiled him up, and ate him for supper, and lived happy ever afterwards.

THE THREE BEARS

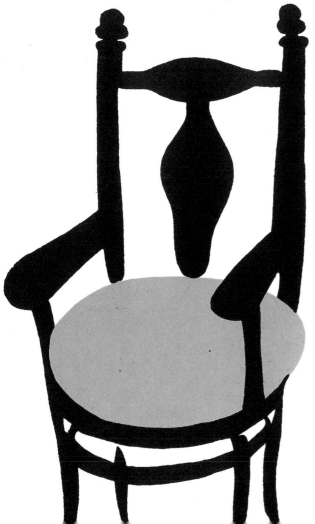

Once upon a time there were Three Bears who lived together in a house at the edge of a wood.   One of them was a Little, Small, Baby Bear ; and one was a Middle-sized Mother Bear; and the other was a Great, Big, Father Bear.   They had each a pot for their porridge : a little pot for the Little, Small, Wee Bear ; and a middle-sized pot for the Middle Bear ; and a great pot for the Great, Big Bear. And they had each a chair to sit in : a little chair for the Little, Small, Wee Bear ; and a middle-sized chair for the Middle Bear ; and a great chair for the Great, Big Bear.   And they had each a bed to sleep in : a little bed for the Little, Small, Wee Bear ; and a middle-sized bed for the Middle Bear ; and a great bed for the Great, Big Bear.

One day after they had made the porridge for their breakfast and poured it into their porridge-pots, they walked out into the wood while the porridge was cooling, that they might not burn their mouths by beginning too soon to eat it.

And while they were walking, a pretty little girl came out of the wood. She saw the dear little house and walked up the little path. First she looked in at the window, and then she peeped in at the keyhole ; and, seeing nobody in the house, she lifted the latch. The door was not fastened, because the Bears were good Bears, who did nobody any harm and never suspected that anyone would harm them. So little Goldilocks opened the door and went in, and well pleased she was when she saw the porridge on the table. If she had been a good, polite little girl, she would have waited till the Bears came home, and then perhaps they would have asked her to breakfast, for they were good Bears—a little rough, as the manner of Bears is, but for all that very good-natured and hospitable. But she was a naughty little girl, and set about helping herself.

So first she tasted the porridge of the Great, Big Bear, and that was too hot for her, and burned her tongue. And then she tasted the porridge of the Middle Bear, and that was too cold for her, and she dropped the spoon on the floor. And then she went to the porridge of the Little, Small, Wee Bear, and tasted that ; and that was neither too hot nor too cold, but just right, and she liked it so well that she ate it all up. Goldilocks was very hungry after her walk in the wood, and the little porridge-pot did not hold enough for her.

Then she sat down in the great big chair of the Great, Big Bear, and that was too hard for her. And then she sat down in the middle-sized chair of the Middle Bear, and that was too soft for her. And then she sat down in the chair of the Little, Small, Wee Bear, and that was neither too hard nor too soft, but just right. So she seated herself in it, and there she sat till the bottom of the chair came out, and down she came, plump, upon the ground. And she was not very pleased about that, I can assure you.

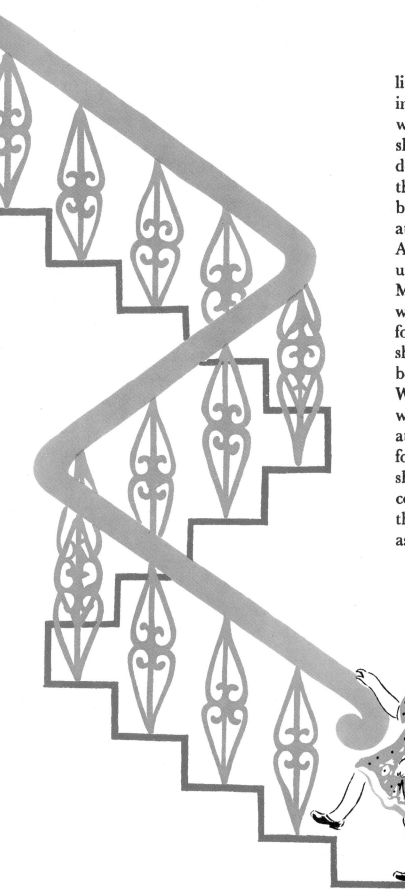

Then this naughty little girl went upstairs into the bed-chamber in which the three Bears slept. And first she lay down upon the bed of the Great, Big Bear; but that was too high at the head for her. And next she lay down upon the bed of the Middle Bear, and that was too high at the foot for her. And then she lay down upon the bed of the Little, Small, Wee Bear, and that was neither too high at the head nor at the foot, but just right. So she covered herself up comfortably and lay there till she fell fast asleep.

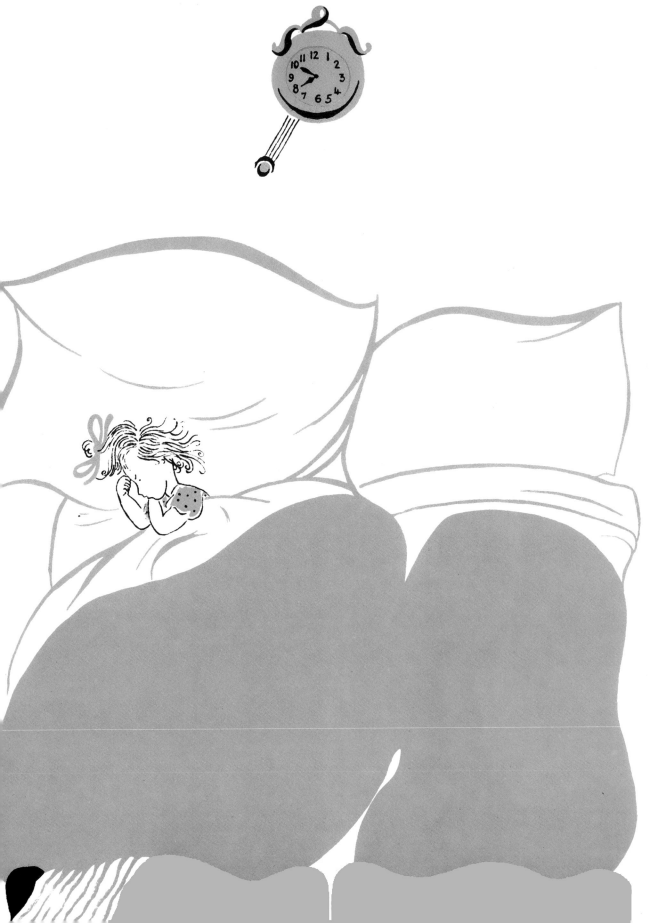

By this time the Three Bears thought their porridge would be cool enough, so they came home to breakfast.

Now Goldilocks has left the spoon of the Great, Big Bear standing in his porridge.

"SOMEBODY HAS BEEN AT MY PORRIDGE!" said the Great, Big Bear, in his great, rough, gruff voice.

And when the Middle Bear looked at hers, she saw that the spoon was lying on the floor. They were wooden spoons, but the floor is not the right place for them, is it?

"*Somebody has been at my porridge!*" said the Middle Bear in her middle voice.

Then the Little, Small, Wee Bear looked at his and there was the spoon in the porridge-pot, but the porridge was all gone.

"Somebody has been at my porridge, and has eaten it all up!" said the Little, Small, Wee Bear, in his little, small, wee voice.

Upon this the Three Bears, seeing that some one had eaten up the Little, Small, Wee Bear's breakfast, began to look about.

Now, Goldilocks had not put the hard cushion straight when she rose from the chair of the Great, Big Bear.

"SOMEBODY HAS BEEN SITTING IN MY CHAIR!" said the Great, Big Bear, in his great, rough, gruff voice.

And naughty Goldilocks had squatted down on the soft cushion of the Middle Bear.

"*Somebody has been sitting in my chair!*" said the Middle Bear, in her middle voice.

And you know what the naughty little girl had done to the third chair.

"Somebody has been sitting in my chair and has sat the bottom out of it!" said the Little, Small, Wee Bear, in his little, small, wee voice.

Then the Three Bears thought that they had better make further search; so they went upstairs into their bed-chamber. Now Goldilocks had pulled the pillow of the Great, Big Bear out of its place.

"SOMEBODY HAS BEEN LYING IN MY BED!"
said the Great, Big Bear, with his great, rough, gruff voice.

And she had pulled the bolster of the Middle Bear out
of its place.

"*Somebody has been lying in my bed!*" said the Middle Bear in
her middle voice.

And when the Little, Small, Wee Bear came to look at his
bed, there was the bolster in its right place and the pillow in
its place upon the bolster; and upon the pillow were spread
the golden curls of a pretty little girl.

"Somebody has been lying in my bed—and here she is!"
said the Little, Small, Wee Bear, in his little, small, wee voice.

Now, Goldilocks had heard in her sleep the great, rough, gruff voice of the Great, Big Bear; but she was so fast asleep that it was no more to her than the roaring of wind or the rumbling of thunder. And she had heard the middle voice of the Middle Bear, but it was only as if she heard some one speaking in a dream.

But when she heard the little, small, wee voice of the Little, Small, Wee Bear, it was so sharp and so shrill that it awakened her at once. Up she started; and when she saw the three Bears on one side of the Bed, she tumbled herself out at the other and ran to the window. Now, the window was open, because the Bears, like good tidy Bears as they were, always opened their bed-chamber window when they got up in the morning.

"STOP HER!" cried the Great, Big Bear in his great, rough, gruff voice.

"*Stop her!*" cried the Middle Bear in her middle voice.

"Stop her!" cried the Little, Small, Wee Bear in his little, small, wee voice.

But Goldilocks jumped out of the window and down the little path, and was swallowed up in the dark wood in the twinkling of an eye.

A Note on Franciszka Themerson

Franciszka Themerson was born in Warsaw, Poland, in 1907 and died in London, England, in 1988. She was essentially a painter, but in Poland during the 1930s she made avant-garde films with her husband, the writer Stefan Themerson, and also illustrated some forty books for children, ten of which were written by Stefan.

Between them the Themersons conjured a distinctive style of engaging children's eyes and minds in the workings of the everyday world (whether the postal system or building a house). The simple tone of their books was untouched by pedagogy and did not patronize. They treated their readers as partners in the discovery of the ordinary rituals, objects, and minutiae of life. And this clarity was matched by the wit, charm, and originality of the design and illustrations of each book. This sort of invention influenced everything the Themersons did together during a lifetime of collaborations.

When the Themersons went to live in Paris, France, in 1938, Franciszka illustrated children's books for the publisher Flammarion. And during the early 1940s, in London, she was again commissioned, this time by Sylvan Press and Harrap, to illustrate stories for children. These included the four published together in 1947 as *My First Nursery Book*, and brought to light again in this volume. In these drawings, for the first time, we see Franciszka exposing traditional English nursery rhymes to some of her more flamboyant graphic inventions.

Franciszka's own favorites among all of the children's books she illustrated were *Through the Looking Glass*, also commissioned by Harrap, but not published until 2001 (Inky Parrot Press), and Stefan Themerson's *Peddy Bottom* (Gaberbocchus Press,1954; third edition, 2003). She was a rarity among modern painters in having devoted so much of her imaginative energy to the entertainment and enlightenment of a young audience.

– Jasia Reichardt
Keeper of the Themerson Estate

Cataloging-in-Publication Data has been applied for and may be obtained from the Library of Congress.

ISBN 978-0-8109-7978-9

Copyright © Franciszka Themerson 1946, 1947, 2008
"A Note on Franciszka Themerson" copyright © Jasia Reichardt 2008
This edition copyright © Tate 2008

First published in 1947
by George G. Harrap & Co. Ltd, London

This edition first published in 2008 by order of the Tate Trustees
by Tate Publishing, a division of Tate Enterprises Ltd, Millbank, London SW1P 4RG
www.tate.org.uk/publishing

Color reprographics by Altaimage, London
Printed and bound in China by C&C Offset Printing Co., Ltd.
10 9 8 7 6 5 4 3 2 1

HNA
harry n. abrams, inc.
a subsidiary of La Martinière Groupe

115 West 18th Street
New York, NY 10011
www.hnabooks.com